Nate the Great
and the
Earth Day
Robot

Nate the Great

and the
Earth Day
Robot

by Andrew Sharmat

illustrated by Olga and Aleksey Ivanov
in the style of Marc Simont

A YEARLING BOOK

This is a work of fiction. Names, characters, places, and incidents either are
the product of the author's imagination or are used fictitiously. Any resemblance
to actual persons, living or dead, events, or locales is entirely coincidental.

New illustrations of Nate the Great, Sludge, Rosamond, Esmeralda, Annie, Claude,
and Harry by Olga and Aleksey Ivanov based upon original drawings by Marc Simont.

Visit us on the Web! rhcbooks.com

Educators and librarians, for a variety of teaching tools, visit us at RHTeachersLibrarians.com

Library of Congress Cataloging-in-Publication Data is available upon request.
ISBN 978-0-593-18083-9 (hardcover) — ISBN 978-0-593-18084-6 (lib. bdg.) —
ISBN 978-0-593-18085-3 (ebook) — ISBN 978-0-593-18086-0 (pbk.)

Printed in the United States of America
10 9 8 7 6 5 4 3 2 1
First Yearling Edition 2022

For Marjorie the Great

Chapter One
Mr. Butler

My name is Nate the Great.

I am a detective.

I am also a student in Mr. Scholari's class in room 236.

Our class project for the Earth Day Fair was a robot.

A small round robot that runs on solar batteries.

The robot's name is Mr. Butler.

Mr. Butler is programmed to vacuum dirt off the floor.

Mr. Butler was invented by Esmeralda.
Esmeralda is the smartest person in the
entire school.

Maybe the entire world.
She is my second-best friend.
My number-one best friend is Sludge,
my dog. Sludge is also a great detective.

But dogs are not allowed at school.
So Esmeralda is my best friend at school.
Whenever someone whistles, Mr. Butler
lights up and shouts, "Cleanup time! Yum-
yum, dirt! Yum-yum, dirt! Yum-yum, dirt!"

His motor starts up.
He rolls across the floor.
He sweeps and vacuums dirt and dust
as he goes.
The dirt and dust disappear into his
compartment.
Mr. Butler loves dirt.
Even more than I love pancakes.
And I, Nate the Great, really love pancakes.
In two days, our class was supposed to
be entering Mr. Butler in the school
Earth Day fair.
There was just one problem.
Mr. Butler had run away.
And nobody knew where he was.

Chapter Two
The Robot Whistler

Mr. Scholari looked unhappy.
"Our Mr. Butler is lost," he said.
Everyone in class turned and looked
at Claude.
Claude is always losing things.
"And we need to find him,"
Mr. Scholari continued.
Everyone in class turned and looked at me.
"I guess I have a new case to solve," I said.
"We know that Mr. Butler was here
yesterday afternoon.

"And he's not here this morning.
Is anyone at
school at night?"
"Only Dusty,
the custodian,"
Mr. Scholari said.
"Then I must
speak to him,"
I said.

"He comes in during the evening,"
Mr. Scholari said.
"Then I need to check the other
classrooms," I said. "I will go on a
search mission."
"Remember that Mr. Butler starts up when
you whistle," Esmeralda said.
"So be sure to whistle while you search."

Chapter Three
Hi-Tech Hex

Ms. Shomer's class is in room 237,
right next to Mr. Scholari's class.
It seemed like a good place to begin
the search.
I introduced myself.
"Class has already started," said Rosamond,
who was seated in front.

"So I will call you Nate the Late."
Rosamond says lots of strange things.
That's because Rosamond is
a strange person.
Rosamond has four cats.
She calls them Big Hex, Little Hex,
Super Hex, and Plain Hex.
I looked around and whistled.
Then everyone whistled.
It was loud.
It sounded horrible.
Suddenly, I heard something else.
Was it Mr. Butler?

"Intruder alert! Intruder alert! MEOW!"
Then I saw something.
It was definitely not Mr. Butler.
It looked like a large robot cat.
It was headed straight for me.
It had a huge camera attached to its
forehead and big claws on its paws.
I, Nate the Great, believe that no one
should run from danger.
I decided to walk.

I decided to walk very quickly.

"Litter box!" shouted Ms. Shomer.

The robot cat stopped and went to a box in the corner of the classroom.

"Sorry about that," Ms. Shomer said.

"This is our project for the Earth Day Fair. It's a robot guard cat."

"Why not a guard dog?" I asked.

I looked at Rosamond.

She was smiling.

"Of course it's a cat," I said.

"How silly of me."

"It was my great, great, great, great idea,"
Rosamond said.

"His name is Hi-Tech Hex. And he is
programmed to guard the classroom.
He knows the faces of everyone in our class.
If strangers come in, he chases them away.
You are a stranger."

"How is that an Earth Day project?" I asked.
Rosamond thought for a moment.

"Well . . ."

She thought for another moment.

"Real cats eat," she finally said.

"Hi-Tech Hex doesn't eat. So there's more food left for the rest of the world. I'm very proud that I am doing my part to help feed the world."

"And the camera?" I asked.

"It records everything that happens here," Ms. Shomer said.

"So we could play back the tape to see if Mr. Butler was here last night," I said.

Chapter Four
Intruder Alert

Ms. Shomer attached Hi-Tech Hex
to a large TV screen.
The video played.
And played.
And played.
Nothing happened.
Suddenly, we saw a man walk in.

He was wearing headphones and had
a bucket and mop.
He was whistling.
It was Dusty.

"Intruder alert! Intruder alert! Meow!"
Dusty looked up.
He screamed.
He ran out of the
classroom.

Hi-Tech Hex raced after him.
"Intruder alert! Intruder alert! Meow!"
yelled the robot.
At the doorway, Hi-Tech Hex stopped.
Then he turned and went back to his
litter box.

Most cats chase mice, I thought.
This one chases custodians.
"Well," said Ms. Shomer, "that explains
the dirty floor."
The video became quiet again.

For a long time, nothing happened.
I was getting ready to move to
the next classroom.
Suddenly, there was another noise.
"Cleanup time! Yum-yum, dirt!"
There was Mr. Butler.
In the video!

Chapter Five
King Klean Vs. Hexzilla

The class continued watching the video.
Mr. Butler had entered the classroom.
His brushes were spinning.
"Yum-yum, dirt! Yum-yum, dirt!
Yum-yum, dirt!"
Mr. Butler was happy.

Hi-Tech Hex was not
happy.
"Intruder alert!
Intruder alert!
Meow!" yelled
Hi-Tech Hex.
He raced toward Mr. Butler.
"Yum-yum, dirt!" shouted Mr. Butler.
But Hi-Tech Hex was not interested in dirt.
Mr. Butler turned toward the door and raced
for the hallway.

"Yum-yum, dirt!" he shouted again.
Hi-Tech Hex chased Mr. Butler into
the hall.
"Intruder alert! Intruder alert! Meow!"
he yelled.
Mr. Butler turned to the right and
went down the hallway.
He went into room 238.
Thanks to Hi-Tech Hex, the case
was solved.
I now knew where I would find Mr. Butler.

Chapter Six
Rustin' in the Rain

In room 238, the class had created
a giant dark cloud.
It was wet in room 238.
It was also hard to see through
the dark cloud.
I realized that Mr. Butler might not
be easy to find.

Mr. Fogg is the teacher in room 238.
He told me that the giant cloud could
be used to keep plants moist.
"It must be hard to get work done in here,"
I said.
"Part of the project is to learn how to live
and work inside the cloud," he said.
Mr. Fogg was wearing a raincoat.

So were all the students.

I, Nate the Great, did not want to live or work inside a cloud.

I wanted to find Mr. Butler and leave as quickly as possible.

"I am looking for a robot vacuum cleaner that our class built," I said.

"His name is Mr. Butler.

Has anybody seen him?"

I could barely see in front of me.

"Or seen anything?"

"There's a new vacuum cleaner in the back of the classroom," said Mr. Fogg.

"I don't remember it being there before."

I walked slowly to the back of the room.

I had to be careful.

It was not easy to see.

Finally, there it was.

The vacuum.

Shiny, squeaky-clean, brand-new.

It was not Mr. Butler.

It was not a robot.

It was just a vacuum cleaner.

I asked the class to whistle.

Then we all listened.

Then whistled again.

Then listened again.

Mr. Butler did not respond.

But why?

I, Nate the Great, knew that the room
was a bad place for Mr. Butler.

He might get wet and rusty.

Then I wouldn't hear him.

Because he would be broken.

It was getting darker inside the cloud, but
Mr. Fogg's class helped me search the room.

There was no trace of Mr. Butler.

I knew that Mr. Butler had entered
room 238, but he was not there anymore.

I had to search the other classrooms.

Chapter Seven
The Garden of Tomorrow

I introduced myself to Mr. Gardner's class in room 239.

Then we all whistled together.

Ms. Shomer's class had sounded horrible when they whistled.

Mr. Gardner's class sounded worse.

"Our class science project," said Mr. Gardner, "is fake soil."

"Why?" I asked.

"A hungry world needs more fertile soil
to grow more vegetables."
Mr. Gardner pointed to several small
containers of soil.
Next to the containers was one large
mound of extra soil.
I looked at the containers.
There were no vegetables growing in
any of them.
I took out my magnifying glass.
I looked carefully in each box.

I, Nate the Great, knew that the only vegetables that would grow in fake soil were fake vegetables.

"How do you make fake soil?" I asked.

"It's a recipe," Mr. Gardner said.

"You need *peat moss* to hold water, *pumice* to hold in the air, *sand* to allow water and air inside, and the magic ingredient: *vermiculite!*"

"That's a funny word," I said.

"What does *ver-mic-u-lite* do?"

"I don't know," Mr. Gardner said.

"But it's in the recipe."

"You should have made pancakes," I said.

"They're easy to make, and they taste better than vegetables.

I'll bet the judges would give you first prize for best-tasting project."

I decided that room 239 was a dead end.

I went to room 240.

Room 240 was Mr. Tierra's class.
In room 240, they
were raising giant,
slimy, disgusting
earthworms.
Yuck!
"Why would
anyone want
giant earthworms?"
I asked.

"Earthworms are
great helpers,"
Mr. Tierra said.
"They allow farmers
to grow more food."
"Maybe they could
help the class in
room 239," I said.

"They're not growing *any* food."
I looked around.
There were giant earthworms crawling
everywhere.
"It looks like you have more earthworms
than you need,"
I said.
I looked
around again.
I noticed there
was also dirt
and mud—
everywhere.
A great place
for Mr. Butler.
A bad place for me.
I searched room 240 as quickly as I could.
There was still no sign of Mr. Butler.
I went from classroom to classroom, seeing
each science project and whistling.

I, Nate the Great,
now had tired lips.
But no Mr. Butler.
It was time to go home and think.

Chapter Eight
The Hound and the Mound

I sat in the backyard with Sludge.
I was eating pancakes.
Sludge was munching a bone.
"Too bad they don't allow dogs in school,"
I said to Sludge.
"I need your help."
Then I told Sludge about Mr. Butler.
And about Hi-Tech Hex in room 237.

And the giant dark cloud in room 238.
And the fake soil in room 239.
And the giant earthworms in room 240.
And all the other science projects in all
the other rooms.

"I should have spent more time in
room 240," I said.
"But the earthworms were everywhere.
Maybe Mr. Butler is in room 240, hiding
from the giant, slimy, disgusting earthworms.
Maybe he's rusted out in room 238.

"It could take years to find him in that cloud. Or maybe he went back to our classroom, where it is much safer.

A classroom without guard cats, dark clouds, earthworms, or *vermiculite*.

Maybe we'll find him there in the morning."

I looked at Sludge.

He was wagging his tail.

"So you think he came back to our classroom?" I asked.

Sludge dug a hole in the ground.

"Are you going to help me with my case?"
I asked. "Or just help me bury that bone?"
Sludge kept digging until there was
a large hole.
And a large mound of dirt.
"Hmmm," I said.
Sludge wagged his tail again.
Then he buried the bone.
But not in the hole.
He buried the bone in the mound of dirt
that was next to the hole.

What a strange thing to do, I thought.
My dog was becoming strange, just like
Rosamond and her cats.

Suddenly, I realized something.
Sludge wasn't strange.
Sludge wasn't strange at all.
Sludge was brilliant!
Sludge had solved the case!
I wrote a note to my mother.

Dear Mother,
Sludge is the
smartest dog.
He deserves an
extra bone.
I must go find
Mr. Butler before
the fair begins.
Love, Nate the Great

Chapter Nine
I Am Not Here to Visit
Your Vegetables

The next morning, I was back in room 236.
I told my class about all the classrooms
I had visited.
"And no sign of Mr. Butler?"
Mr. Scholari asked.
"None," I said.
"I couldn't find him anywhere."
"So he's still lost," Claude said.

"Not for long," I said.
"My dog, Sludge, knows where he is.
And I, Nate the Great, will bring him
back to room 236."
I walked out the door.
I walked down the hall.
I walked past room 237.
I walked past room 238.
I stopped at room 239.
And I went inside.

This time I saw something amazing.
There were vegetables
growing in all
of the boxes.
Corn, cauliflower,
onions, and lettuce.

Red peppers,
green peppers,
orange peppers, and
yellow peppers.
Even blue peppers.

I had never
seen blue
peppers before.

"How did this all grow overnight?" I asked.

Mr. Gardner shrugged.

"I have no idea," he said.

"Must be the vermiculite."

"I'm impressed," I said.

"But I, Nate the Great, am not here to visit your vegetables.

I am here to visit the mound of soil *next* to the vegetables."

I bent down and started digging into the
mound of fake soil.
Nothing yet.
I kept digging.
Still nothing.
I dug some more.
At last, I felt something.
Something plastic, and metal, and round.
I pulled out the plastic and metal
and round thing.
It was Mr. Butler!
Mr. Butler was buried in the mound of soil.
Mr. Butler looked sick.

"Are you okay?" I asked.

I whistled.

Mr. Butler made a strange noise.

"Clean . . . up . . . time," he groaned softly.

Mr. Butler burped.

Then his light went out.

Mr. Butler's solar-powered batteries
had run down.
And his compartment was stuffed
with fake dirt.
Mr. Butler would need a battery charge
and a good cleaning.

Chapter Ten
Dirt, Cats, Earthworms, Clouds, and Blue Peppers

It was the morning of the Earth Day Fair. All the classes were in the gym with their science projects.

Mr. Butler was now cleaned up.

His solar-powered batteries were freshly charged.

"Are you ready?" I asked.

I whistled.

"Cleanup time! Yum-yum, dirt! Yum-yum, dirt! Yum-yum, dirt!" Mr. Butler shouted. He was ready.

"Our guard cat is going to win first prize," Rosamond said.

"He's very high-tech.
But Mr. Butler can clean our classroom floor
after we win."
"Yum-yum, dirt!" Mr. Butler shouted.
"I understand how Mr. Butler found the pile
of dirt," Esmeralda said.
"But why did he start up in the first place?
There is nobody in the room at night."
"But there is," I said.
"The custodian cleans the classrooms
every night.
Dusty listens to loud music through his
headphones.
And he whistles to the music."
"So he set off Mr. Butler by whistling,"
Esmeralda said.

"And the music was so loud that he never heard Mr. Butler turn on," I said.

The fair started.

Three judges went over to the guard cat.

"This is Hi-Tech Hex," Rosamond said proudly.

"He will see that you are strangers and
chase you away."
But Hi-Tech Hex didn't chase
the judges away.
Rosamond pushed buttons.
Nothing happened.

"The guard cat is programmed to protect
room 237," I whispered to Esmeralda.
"I don't think he will work in the gym."

Next up was Mr. Butler.

Esmeralda poured a trail of dirt on the floor.

Then she whistled.

Mr. Butler turned on.

"Cleanup time!" he shouted.

"Yum-yum, dirt! Yum-yum, dirt!

Yum-yum, dirt!"

He started cleaning the trail of dirt.
The judges clapped their hands.
"Bravo! Bravo!" Judge Number One said.
When Mr. Butler finished with the trail,
he continued to clean the gym floor.

The judges looked at the other class
projects.
They looked at the giant, slimy earthworms.
They looked at the huge dark cloud that
was starting to spread across the gym.
Finally, they reached the fake soil.
By now the vegetables had grown huge.
"I've never seen veggies this big,"
said Judge Number Three.
"And I've never seen a blue pepper
before," said Judge Number Two.
Each of the judges took a bite of
a blue pepper.

"Delicious," Judge Number One said.
The judges huddled together.

"First place in this year's Earth Day Fair
goes to Mr. Gardner's class for their artificial
soil," said Judge Number Two.
"They also get first place for best-tasting
project."

But not everyone was hungry for
blue peppers.
At that moment, someone whistled, and
Mr. Butler headed straight for Mr. Gardner's
fake-soil vegetables.

"Cleanup time! Yum-yum, dirt! Yum-yum, dirt! Yum-yum, dirt!" Mr. Butler shouted. He plowed straight into room 239's science project and began gulping up the fake soil. "Yum-yum, dirt! Yum-yum, dirt! Yum-yum, dirt!" he shouted again.

Before anyone could stop him, he had sucked up all the soil.

He left the vegetables untouched.

Then the giant cloud spread across the gym.
The gym turned dark.

"Intruder alert! Intruder alert! Meow!"
yelled Hi-Tech Hex.

"So Hi-Tech Hex *does* work outside of room 237," Esmeralda said.

"Hmmm," I said.

"Maybe it's so dark that he can't tell where he is."

"Hi-Tech Hex!" Esmeralda laughed. "A cat who guards against custodians, vacuum cleaners, and dark clouds!"

"I prefer Low-Tech Sludge," I said. "A dog who finds bones and solves mysteries!"

～Extra～
Fun Activities!

What's Inside

Mr. Butler cleans up dirt. Nate wanted to know more about other robots and how they help people. Here's what he learned.

NATE'S NOTES: The Work Robots Do

Robots can be insect-sized. One called RoboBee can fly. Someday, RoboBee may help plants grow, like bees do.

Robots can be big. Just for fun, people in Japan built a robot nearly sixty feet tall. It can move its legs, arms, hands, and feet.

Many robots can swim. They are used to explore the ocean and study marine animals.

Some robots make pancakes!

Robots have visited Mars. The red
planet is cold, at -80° Fahrenheit on
average, and the flight alone would
take at least a year, round trip,
which is why humans haven't been
there yet.

The Mars robots are called rovers. But they don't look like dogs. They are nearly the size of a regular car, but they have six wheels!

A rover landed on Mars in 2021. It beams photos back to Earth. It is also picking up rocks and dirt. These samples will arrive on Earth around 2031.

Archytas of Tarentum, a mathematician, built what is considered the first robot in history: a mechanical bird propelled by compressed air. This happened around the fifth century BCE.

R2-D2—of Star Wars fame—is the only character to appear unchanged and not grow old throughout the film series!

How to Grow Your Own Sprouts Almost Overnight

The students in Room 239 grew vegetables in boxes. You can grow sprouts almost as fast. No fake soil needed!

Ask an adult to help you.

GET TOGETHER:

- seeds or dried beans or lentils
- a glass jar
- a T-shirt you don't want
- scissors
- a rubber band
- water

GROW YOUR SPROUTS:

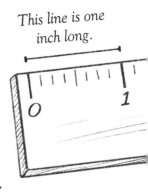

This line is one inch long.

1. Cut a square out of the T-shirt. Make the square at least one inch bigger than the jar opening on all sides.
2. Add a handful of seeds to the jar.
3. Add water to cover the seeds.
4. Cover your jar's opening with the fabric. Use the rubber band to hold it in place.
5. Wait overnight. Pour the water out through the fabric covering. That will stop the seeds from falling out.
6. Two times a day, add water to the jar. Pour it out right away. Keep the seeds damp but not wet.
7. After three days, your seeds should sprout.
8. Now they are ready to eat! Keep them cold in the fridge.

You can put sprouts on a sandwich! Or eat them in salad.

11

Funny Pages

Q: Why did the robot get upset?
A: *Everyone was pushing its buttons.*

Q: What's worse than finding a worm in your apple?
A: *Finding half of a worm in your apple.*

Q: What did one snowperson say to another?
A: *Do you smell carrots?*

A word about learning with
Nate The Great

The Nate the Great series is good fun and has been entertaining children for over forty years. These books are also valuable learning tools in and out of the classroom.

Nate's world—his home, his friends, his neighborhood—is one that every young person recognizes. Nate introduces beginning readers and those who have graduated to early chapter books to the detective mystery genre, and they respond to Nate's commitment to solving the case and helping his friends.

What's more, as Nate the Great solves his cases, readers learn with him. Nate unravels mysteries by using evidence collection, cogent reasoning, problem-solving, analytical skills, and logic in a way that teaches readers to develop critical-thinking abilities. The stories help children start discussions about how to approach difficult situations and give them tools to resolve them.

When you read a Nate the Great book with a child, or when a child reads a Nate the Great mystery on his or her own, the child is guaranteed a satisfying ending that will have taught him or her important classroom and life skills. We know that you and your children will enjoy reading and learning from Nate the Great's wonderful stories as much as we do.

Happy reading and learning with Nate!

Solve all the mysteries with

Nate the Great

ANDREW SHARMAT previously collaborated with his mother, Marjorie Weinman Sharmat, the creator of Nate the Great. Now Andrew continues solving mysteries with Nate and Sludge in *Nate the Great and the Earth Day Robot*, his first solo Nate the Great mystery. He lives in Indiana.

OLGA AND ALEKSEY IVANOV are renowned children's book illustrators and classically trained commercial artists. This talented husband-and-wife team immigrated to the United States in 2002 and found their home, #hylandstudio, in the Rocky Mountains in Colorado. In all, the two have illustrated over one hundred children's books.

ivanovillustration.com